Winner, Winner, Turkey Dinner

LUCKY LUKE'S HUNTING ADVENTURES

by Kevin Lovegreen

Illustrated by Margarita Sikorskaia

ISBN 13: 978-0-9857179-2-6

Printed in the United States of America

First Printing: 2012

16 15 14 13 12   5 4 3 2 1

Cover and interior design by James Monroe Design, LLC.

Lucky Luke, LLC.
4335 Matthew Drive
Eagan, Minnesota 55123

LuckyLukeHunting.com

Quantity discounts available!

*This book is dedicated to my
turkey hunting buddies, old and new.
Thank you for your friendship
and the life long memories.*

Chapter 1

"I was back in the valley just as the light was beginning to break and I heard a booming gobble. I quickly moved in that direction, trying to track down that turkey. When I felt like I was getting close to where that gobble came from, I slowed down to listen and scan for movement. After a minute or two, I didn't see or hear anything, so I pulled out my turkey call and made a couple of hen yelps. Instantly he gobbled again. And that gobble helped me pin-point the giant pine tree he was roosted in. I was within 80 yards of him and I figured that was close enough. I didn't want to try to get any closer and take the chance of getting busted. The sun was rising and I knew he would be leaving his roost soon. I set up my hen decoy in a little opening and snuck back into the woods and got ready.

"When I made another call he gobbled again and I knew he thought a hen was waiting for him. Then I heard wings flapping and a thud. My heart started pounding, because he was on the ground. With any luck, he was coming my way. A loud cawing crow flew over and he lit up and gobbled again, and I could hear him coming closer. I made two quiet yelps and he lit up again and then I could see his head through the brush. It was awesome. I had my gun up on my knee, I was perfectly still. I was ready. When he saw my decoy he suddenly puffed up, fanned his tail, and stuck his head out and gobbled. He was so close and loud I swear I could feel the air from his beak blowing in my face. All fanned out, he marched in and circled my decoy like a sumo wrestler circling his opponent. I made one cluck sound with my mouth call. Right then, he stuck his head up, and BAM, I dropped him. It was one of the best hunts I've ever had."

That night at the dinner table, as Dad told us the story of how he called that big turkey into his decoy, I could picture myself sitting right next to him. I dreamed it was me getting ready to take the shot.

"Hey Luke, back to earth, your vegetables are waiting," Mom said with a smile.

"Yeah, I know, I just can't wait to get my own turkey one day," I said, loading a fork full of green beans.

"I'll make a deal with you, Luke. You clear the table tonight and do the dishes, and I'll bring you along next year. How does that sound?" Dad asked.

"Yes! That sounds great! Is everyone done?"

"Hold your horses, young man, we aren't done yet," Mom said, shaking her head.

Chapter 2

The next spring, not long after my tenth birthday, Dad's story was still playing back in my mind as I helped him pack in our crowded little hunting room. I was finally going turkey hunting and I had a million questions. Luckily for me, my dad had all the answers.

Dad showed me the three decoys we were going to use. There were two hens and one jake (a young tom). He said the big toms can't stand it when the jakes are near a hen during the spring breeding season. He also showed me the different calls that he was going to use. He had a slate call that sounds just like a hen turkey. It's round and has a clay-like slate material in the middle.

You use a wood or plastic striker, about the size of a pencil, to scratch the surface and make the sounds. I practice with the slate call a lot and am getting pretty good at sounding like a turkey.

Dad's other hen call is a mouth call. It fits in your mouth and you squeeze it between your tongue and the roof of your mouth. I can't get that one to work very well. Dad says it takes a lot of practice and I believe him. Until I get better, I will let him do the calling with the mouth call.

"Can the turkeys smell us, like deer can?" I asked.

Dad joked, "They already can see like a hawk. If they could smell like a deer, we would probably never get one!"

We pulled out our guns from the gun safe and carefully slid them into their cases. My gun is a 20-gauge pump and it fits me perfectly. It has a nice walnut stock and I keep it clean as a whistle. Dad grabbed the box of #4 shells for me and we put them into the shell box.

Last fall when we were up at the cabin, Dad set up targets with turkey heads on them. Dad wanted me to get used to shooting the strong turkey shells. Those turkeys are tough, and they have really thick layers of feathers, so we have to shoot powerful loads at them. We tried shooting #4 and #5 size shot to see which one shot a better pattern out of my 20-gauge. Besides kicking really hard and surprising me each time, the

#4 shells shot a better pattern and really covered the turkey's neck and head on the target. "Those #4s are going to do the trick!" Dad said with a smile.

We spent the whole afternoon going through camo clothes, masks, gloves, boots, and other turkey hunting gear. I love hanging out with Dad in the hunting room.

Chapter 3

The lucky weekend finally came, and the truck was packed. Before we left, Dad laid out a map on the table to show me our driving route and pointed out the area where we would be hunting. Dad explained, "Years ago, my friend Mel and I saw an ad in a newspaper. A farmer was advertising hunting land for rent, and we immediately called him up. After we both bagged turkeys on that first hunt, we have been going there almost every spring."

We were excited to get going, so we gave Mom a hug and jumped in our big silver truck. Off we went, heading for the southeast corner of Minnesota. After a long drive, and lots of turkey-hunting talk, we turned off the blacktop and drove down a curved dirt driveway. We pulled up to a farm with a big red barn on the right and a tall white house on the left. By the look of the weathered wood on both, I figured they had to be really old. There was cool old, rusted farm equipment everywhere I looked.

We had the windows down as we drove in, looking for turkeys, so Dad's red hair was a little messy as he slid on his baseball cap. I smiled, because we were wearing matching lucky hats, each with a turkey on the front.

We walked over to the barn, where we heard the sound of steel clanging. There was the farmer, all covered in grease, working on a huge tractor. He saw us and stopped what he was doing. He pulled a rag from his back pocket and cleaned off his hands as he walked over.

The farmer shook my dad's hand. "It's good to see you. And who do we have here?" he asked, nodding at me.

"This is Luke. Luke, this is John," my dad said.

I shook John's hand and couldn't believe how rough and strong it was. And huge! It was like shaking hands with a giant. He had a grease smudge on his cheek, and I wasn't sure if I should tell him about it or not.

"Nice to meet you," I said with a smile. "This is my first turkey hunt and I can't wait to get out there and try to get one. I'm a really good shot and my dad and I have been doing a lot of practicing. Have you seen many turkeys?"

John's eyebrows raised and with a growing smile he said, "I can see someone is excited to go hunting. There are plenty of turkeys around. It's up to you to get one."

"Have you been seeing them in the usual spots?" Dad asked.

"For the most part. I have seen them a couple of mornings behind the old pasture," John said. "You always seem to have good luck back in the valley. I would think that's where you should try first."

"Dad has told me so many stories about seeing turkeys back in the valley that I can't wait to go there tomorrow morning," I piped in.

"You stick with your dad and I have a feeling he will find you a turkey. I better get back to work—that tractor isn't going to fix itself. You can head around back to the old trailer house where you'll be staying."

Dad and I hopped in the truck and drove to the back of the farm. As we were pulling up to the trailer house, Dad suddenly stopped the truck.

"Look at that!" Dad said with excitement.

I looked out the window and there were ten wild turkeys standing in the field just past the trailer. I don't think my eyes could have gotten any bigger. There were seven hens and three giant toms, the adult male turkeys.

"See how the toms are all fanned out?" Dad asked.

"Yep," I answered.

"That's their way of showing off to the girl turkeys," Dad explained.

"Cool! They sure are huge!" I said.

After watching for a while, we eased closer to the trailer. The turkeys finally saw the truck, and it was like someone had blown a warning alarm. They all put their heads down and ran up the hill into the woods. I couldn't believe how fast they could move!

"That was exciting," Dad said with a smile. "It's unfortunate our season starts tomorrow. We could have gone after them. I have never seen turkeys that close to the trailer before."

We unpacked the truck and brought our gear into the trailer. It was surprisingly clean for such an old place. There was a kerosene heater in the living room with two little couches that had pictures of running deer on them. The kitchen floor was faded yellow, and the little table had two printed maps of the property on it, along with a lantern.

"What's the lantern for?" I asked Dad.

"For light! There's no electricity in the trailer. We're roughing it," he said with a smile.

We laid out our gear on the living room floor so we would be ready for the early morning.

After dinner we headed to the little back bedroom. I climbed into the top bunk, where my favorite sleeping bag was waiting, and Dad turned out the lantern and slid into the bottom bunk. At first it was so dark I couldn't see the ceiling two feet above me. Then my eyes adjusted, and the moonlight filled the room with a soft glow.

It took me a long time to get to sleep because I couldn't stop thinking about all the turkeys we had seen. By the sound of Dad's snoring, he didn't have any trouble at all falling asleep.

Chapter 4

I must have finally dozed off, because the sound of the alarm clock startled me.

"It's turkey time! You ready?" Dad asked.

"You betcha!" I said through a yawn.

We crawled out of our sleeping bags, and Dad lit the lantern. I realized then that my eyes weren't quite ready to wake up. "What time is it?" I asked.

"It's 4:30. Part of turkey hunting is getting up early."

We made our way to the living room and I pulled on my clothes. I slipped on my boots without tying them and went outside to go to the bathroom. I took a long, deep breath, and the cool morning air felt good in my lungs. I looked up into the sky, and it was crystal clear. There were a million stars out, and the moon was bright. Not knowing if there were any skunks or raccoons around made it a little spooky walking over to the outhouse. I creaked the door open and waited a second, listening for anything moving inside. When I knew the coast was clear, I stepped in and used one foot to prop the door open a bit to let a little moonlight in. When I was done, I scampered back to the trailer where the light from the lantern— and my dad, of course—were a relief.

"You survived?" Dad joked.

"Yep, all good, and no critters got me."

After a quick bowl of cereal and a mouthwatering chocolate doughnut, we tied up our boots and out the door we went.

With our shotguns slung over our shoulders, we marched across a cut corn field. At the other end of the field, we headed down a trail that went into the woods. After a few minutes of walking, we came to an area in a ravine that opened up a bit. Dad stopped and put his mouth close to my ear.

"We are going to set up here," he whispered. "Go sit next to that tree, and I will put out the decoys. Be very quiet; the turkeys might be close."

"Okay," I whispered back. I snuck over to the tree and sat down.

I watched as Dad walked out to the middle of the opening and slid three turkey decoys from his vest. He carefully opened them up and stuck them on stakes that he pushed into the ground. He snuck back to where I was and sat down next to me.

Dad took my gun and slid two shells in.

"The safety is on. You're ready to go," Dad said quietly as he handed the gun back to me.

He loaded his gun and laid it down next to him. We pulled on our face masks and Dad gave me a thumbs up.

Dad told me there is a time in the morning, as the sun is coming up, that the toms will gobble at just about any loud sound. That blows the turkeys' cover and lets us know where they are. I couldn't wait to hear that first gobble.

There are a few tricks that turkey hunters use to get the toms to gobble in the morning. Most of them are calls that are supposed to get the turkeys to respond. Hunters usually use crow calls, owl calls, or hen calls.

Dad made a few quiet hen calls, but we didn't hear a response. In the spring, when the toms hear the hen call, they usually gobble at it. Especially when they are just waking up perched high on a big tree branch.

We sat quietly for a few minutes, and then it started. It was just like someone tapped the turkeys on the shoulder and woke them up. At the far end of the valley, a turkey gobbled. That started a chain reaction. I could hear the gobbles getting closer and closer until two gobbled right behind us. I couldn't believe it! Those gobbles were one of the coolest sounds I have ever heard. It's hard to explain how a gobble sounds, but it kind of sounds like someone yelling as they shake their head and flap their loose cheeks.

I pushed my back into the tree, trying to blend in. Dad's eyes lit up, and I could tell he was smiling under his mask. He started nodding his head and pointed with his thumb. "They're right behind us," Dad whispered with excitement.

Dad picked up his turkey call again and made a couple of hen sounds. The two toms behind us gobbled instantly. Dad's eyes lit up again. I think he was proud he made them gobble.

"They think a hen is here—that's good!" Dad said.

The morning light began to fill the woods, and it was like magic. All kinds of birds were singing along with the turkeys gobbling, and the green of the grass looked like it was glowing. Watching the morning light wake up the forest and the animals is one of the best things about being in the woods bright and early.

As the sun shined through the trees with more intensity, I tried but I couldn't see the tops of the two big hills in front of us. If a turkey were gobbling from up there, it would take us a long time to get in range. The trail where we walked in was alongside an old, dried-up river that carved through the bottom of the ravine. The hillsides were covered with shades of green from the new spring leaves popping out.

Suddenly, a cawing crow making its morning rounds flew over us, which made every turkey in the woods gobble. It seemed like they were yelling at the crow to get out of *their* woods! As the sun peeked over the trees at the end of the valley, the turkeys gobbled with more intensity. Then we heard some hens yelping behind us. That really got the toms going crazy!

It startled me when I heard the turkeys flapping their wings, each landing on the ground with a *THUD*. Dad put his hand on my leg and whispered, "Don't move, keep your eyes open."

The hens yelped again and the toms instantly gobbled in response. They sounded like they were right behind us. With my head perfectly still, I kept trying to look out of the corner of my eyes to see any movement. Dad made a yelp sound from his call and the toms gobbled back. My heart pounded, and the excitement was building. It was like opening day of a new movie, with the previews over and the screen black—I was ready for the big show to begin. After a couple of thrilling minutes, we realized the turkeys had other plans. We could hear the hens calling and the toms gobbling, but they were getting farther and farther away.

Dad shook his head. "The hens took our toms away. It happens all the time. Wow, was that amazing or what?"

"That was so cool! I thought I was going to get one of those gobblers," I said.

"I did too. But hearing them and getting that close is half the fun. We'll just sit here for a while and see if they come back," Dad said.

We sat for the next hour and could hear turkeys gobbling off in the distance, but nothing came in. The periods of silence gave me plenty of time to daydream about a turkey coming close. It was also kind of nice to hang out with Dad and have things so peaceful and quiet. At home we are always running around doing something, and it seems like we never slow down.

"I guess we have to pick up the decoys and go find a gobbler," Dad said.

"Let's do it, I'm ready for some action!"

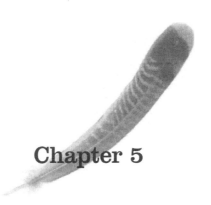

Chapter 5

We headed farther down the trail, stopping every few minutes to try a call, hoping a tom would respond. It wasn't long before we heard a turkey gobble just up the hill from us. Dad looked at me. "Let's go get him." We hurried up the hill and found a spot that opened up to a plateau. We waited there and Dad used his mouth call to make three yelp sounds. The tom gobbled back. We could tell he was just over a knoll from us. We quickly sat down and Dad told me to get my gun ready. I couldn't believe how fast things were happening. The turkey gobbled again and then I could hear him drumming. It's a really weird and cool sound. It sort of sounds like someone dropping marshmallows on a big Indian drum. The drumming went on and on, and every time Dad called, the turkey would gobble. I just knew that at any moment the tom would peek over the ridge. This went on for about 15 minutes and I was going crazy. "Belly crawl up and see if you can get a shot. He's not going to come in," Dad whispered. I was ready to try anything, so on my belly I went.

Like an army guy with my gun in front of me, I slowly made my way through the brush, trying not to make any noise. I heard the turkey drum again and knew he was still there, just out of my sight. As I broke the crest and could finally see the other side, I searched with all my might to catch a glance of the turkey. Scanning from left to right, and then right to left, I looked everywhere. But that turkey wasn't there. I couldn't believe he was gone! I had just heard him only moments earlier. I finally eased up to my knees so I could see more and waited. Nothing!

I turned and looked at Dad with my arms out, shaking my head. "He's gone!" I said in a loud whisper.

"Isn't it crazy how they can sneak off like that? He must have heard or seen you," Dad said. "Well, you did your best and gave it a try. Let's get back to the trail and keep heading down the valley. You never know when our luck will change."

Chapter 6

Slowly making our way down the trail, calling every couple minutes, I hoped for more action. Suddenly, we heard a turkey gobble echo through the woods. We froze in our tracks. Dad pointed his finger up and turned his head, as if trying to hear a pin drop. To our surprise, the tom gobbled again and we both turned our heads to look. Dad pointed his finger in the direction of the gobble and said, "Bingo! It sounds like it's coming from the old logging road up ahead. Let's get up there and check it out!"

As we hurried down the trail trying to close the distance, not just one but two or three turkeys started gobbling. We slowed down as we approached the old road. "Wait here and I will take a look," Dad said, a little out of breath.

He handed me his gun and crawled to the edge of the opening. After taking a peek, he quickly pulled back and gave me a thumbs up. In a hurry, he pulled one hen decoy out of his vest. He balanced the decoy on the stake and eased it out into the trail. He reached his arm out as far as he could without revealing his body, being careful so the turkeys didn't see him. As soon as the decoy was stuck in the ground the turkeys began to gobble louder and faster.

"Hurry up! We need to get ready. They're coming!" Dad explained.

My heart was pounding as we scurried back into the woods and sat down next to a huge, dead tree.

From the moment Dad put out the decoy, the turkeys didn't stop gobbling. They kept getting louder and louder. I had my 20-gauge shotgun balanced on my left knee and kept my eyes peeled for any movement. "Take a couple deep breaths and calm down," Dad advised. I think he could see my chest pounding. I tried to take a deep breath, and as I did, my eyes just about popped out of my head. I finally saw my first turkey live in the woods while I was on a hunt, and it was walking right down the trail like he was on a mission, heading for our decoy.

"There he is! Don't move a muscle. Just let him come," Dad whispered in my ear.

As I watched in amazement, trying to play out in my mind what was going to happen, another turkey appeared behind the first one. I couldn't believe it—two turkeys!

And then I heard the most amazing gobble of all come from behind the second turkey. It was so loud it felt like it vibrated my whole body.

"The big one is behind the first two. Let them go by and see if you can take the big one," Dad whispered.

"K," was all I could muster up. I'm not sure I could have spoken full words if I'd tried.

As the first two turkeys cleared the brush and walked into the opening in front of us, I could tell by their small beards they were jakes. For a chance at that big tom, I was willing to pass on the young birds. To my surprise, the turkeys immediately turned and looked right at me. My heart was racing, and I could hear Dad whispering, "Don't move, don't move, they see you moving." The jakes started to get really nervous, and their heads were popping around like they were on springs.

Suddenly, I realized the end of my gun was shaking. I tried to hold it steady, but it was getting heavy because I had lifted it off my knee. When I slowly lowered my gun to balance it back on my left knee, the turkeys became super nervous. They knew something wasn't right with Dad and me, but they really wanted to go past us to check out the hen decoy.

At that moment I finally caught a glimpse of the big tom. I could see his right eye peeking through the brush trying to see what was causing the two jakes to be so nervous. Then the first two started to cluck—the turkeys' warning call. I didn't know how much time I had before they ran off.

I tried to take slow, deep breaths to calm down, but it wasn't working. I started talking to myself, like Dad told me he does when he's trying to calm his nerves. *Relax. You've got this. Wait for the big one to show. When you see him, click the safety off, lift the gun, aim, and take him.*

So quiet I could hardly hear it, my dad said, "Get ready. There he is."

And then it happened. Just as the two jakes were turning to leave, the big tom poked his head around the bush and appeared.

"Take him, take him!" Dad whispered urgently.

In one motion, I clicked the safety off and raised my gun. I quickly aimed at the turkey's head and pulled the trigger. *BANG!* The gun rang out.

"You got him, you got him!" Dad howled.

We both jumped up and ran to the road. The two jakes were running like Big Bird from *Sesame Street*, right down the middle of the trail. The giant tom was on his back, with his feet sticking up in the air.

"You did it, buddy! Way to go! And it was a perfect shot." Dad was beaming.

"YES! Woohoo!" I yelled as I ran over to the tom.

I kept my gun ready just in case he got up and tried to run away. I quickly realized he wasn't going anywhere, so I clicked my safety on and hurried back to Dad.

"Now that's what I'm talking about!" I said as I high-fived Dad.

"Look how big he is!" Dad said in amazement.

"He's a giant!" I agreed.

"You did an awesome job holding it together. All your practice shooting paid off. I'm so proud of you, Luke. You're a great hunter."

"Thanks, Dad," I said proudly. "I just wasn't sure what those jakes were going to do and if they were going to scare the big tom away. I tried really hard to keep my gun steady but man, it was hard."

"You played it out perfectly, and every hunt is different. Sometimes a turkey takes off from seeing a little movement and other times they get so excited about the decoy you can move and they don't pay any attention. That's one thing that makes turkey hunting so much fun—and so challenging," Dad said. As we captured the adventure by taking a bunch of pictures, we kept re-telling parts of the hunt over and over to each other.

I couldn't wait to tell Mom the good news, so on the way back I called her up. I went on and on, telling her every detail. I could tell by her voice she was really excited for me. "You and Dad sure make a good team. I'm proud of you, Luke, and I'm glad you're having such a good time," she said.

We went back to the trailer house and weighed and measured the turkey. He weighed twenty-five pounds, had one-and-a-half-inch spurs on his legs, and had a thirteen-inch beard. He was a true trophy.

We drove around to the farmhouse where John was doing some chores. I quickly jumped out and ran over to him.

"Excuse me, John. Sorry for interrupting your work. Would you have a minute to come and look at what I got this morning?" I asked with excitement. He stopped what he was doing, raised his eyebrows and looked at me.

"I can't wait to see," he said with a smile. He stood up and followed me over to the truck.

"Check out this beauty," I said proudly. He looked in the back of the truck and grinned so wide his eyes squinted.

"That's one nice turkey, young man. Your dad told me that you were lucky, and he wasn't kidding."

"I sure am. Thank you very much for allowing us to hunt on your farm. This place is amazing!"

"Well, I'm glad you had fun and that you got yourself such a nice bird. Now you have to help your dad get *his* turkey," he said with a wink.

"I will see what I can do about that this afternoon," I promised.

Chapter 7

We went back to the trailer for a quick lunch and a well-deserved nap. When we woke, we headed back out in hopes of getting Dad his turkey. "We will head up to the corn field on top of the bluff. The turkeys like to come out in the corn and feed before roosting for the evening," Dad explained.

We parked the truck on the side of the road, halfway up a big hill. Dad grabbed his gun out of the case and we hiked up the hill and across the big field. "We will set up in the far corner; in the past this has been a great spot to see birds," Dad said. We set up all three decoys and found a couple of big trees to sit next to. I was the caller tonight, because I had already bagged my bird. We sat for a while and then I tried my slate call to make a few hen yelps. I will admit the first few calls were not my best. It was a little harder out in the field because I wanted each one to sound perfect. I relaxed a little and then the call started to sound just like a hen turkey. Dad gave me thumbs up, and that made me feel good. All my practicing was paying off. I really wanted to help Dad get a turkey.

We didn't hear or see anything for about an hour. But then like a rabbit popping out of a hat, there was a hen eating about 60 yards away. Hoping to get her attention, I made a soft yelp sound with my call, and she put her head up and looked over at us. When she saw the decoys she looked for a long time and then started walking over. She seemed very curious and within minutes she was standing right in the middle of the three decoys. I got the feeling she couldn't understand why they weren't moving or making any noise. Then she lost interest in the decoys and started picking at the ground for bugs and moved closer to us. She ended up about three steps in front of me and I could see every detail of her awesome feathers. Even though we could only shoot tom turkeys, my heart was beating hard, having her that close. She turned and took her time pecking her way out to the middle of the field. "That was really cool," I whispered.

"That sure was. She had no idea we were here. She also couldn't figure out why her friends didn't want to hang out with her." Dad grinned.

Suddenly my eyes opened wide. "Look over there!"

Not wanting to make any movement with my hands, I stared across the field. Dad followed my eyes and locked on the turkey. "That's a nice bird!" Dad whispered. A giant tom with a long beard was standing about 80 yards away, scanning the field. "Hit the call and see what he does," Dad said.

"Okay, I'll give it a try," I said, excited to put my practice to the test. I used my striker to scratch the slate and a perfect *Yelp Yelp Yelp* rang from the call. The tom stretched his neck high and looked right over at our setup. He gobbled once and put his head down and started running over to our decoys. I couldn't believe my eyes. "It worked!" I whispered to Dad.

"It sure did, let's see what happens here."

Dad had his elbows balanced on his knees and his gun ready. I was sitting just to his left and had the best seat in the house. The tom stopped about 40 yards away and puffed up and started drumming. Then the wind picked up and caused the jake decoy to spin on its post. That was all it took. The tom put his feathers down and ran over to the jake and attacked it. I couldn't believe what was happening! And I couldn't believe Dad wasn't shooting! Once the jake decoy fell over, the tom jumped on it. Then he puffed up and started marching over to the hen decoy on the left. He circled it, walking in an awkward sideways march. He clearly was trying to show off to our decoy. Then without warning, another tom came running in from behind us and ran right up to the first tom and attacked him. It was an all-out turkey brawl and it was happening right in front of us.

I heard Dad click his safety off, and with his mouth call, he made a loud cluck sound. Both turkeys stopped fighting, gobbled back and puffed up. At that moment Dad's gun rang out and the tom on the right dropped in his tracks. "YES! Nice shot!" I yelled. We didn't have to be quiet anymore—we both had our turkeys. We jumped up, high fived, and watched as the other tom ran for his life across the field.

"That was awesome! Why did you wait so long to take him?" I asked.

"I wanted you to get a good show, and boy those turkeys did their job," Dad said, smiling from ear to ear. "Wasn't that something? Can you believe that other turkey came out of nowhere to beat up that first tom? I definitely didn't see that coming."

"The whole thing was just amazing to watch. You put the smackdown on that big tom," I said.

"We will definitely be going into town tonight to have a celebration dinner. Nice calling, by the way. Just like a professional guide, you brought him right in with that slate call," Dad said.

"Thanks!" I said, bursting with pride.

Dad picked up the decoys and I heaved the tom over my shoulder for the walk back. That thing was huge, and my shoulder was aching by the time we got back to the truck. I took several pictures of Dad and his turkey. His bird weighed twenty-one pounds, had one-inch spurs and a ten-inch beard. I had Dad beat in all categories, but his bird was still a beauty, definitely one to be proud of.

After cleaning up and changing our clothes, we headed into town for a juicy burger.

On the way back to the farm after dinner, I called my buddy Jack up to tell him about our fantastic day. Jack and his dad have never been turkey hunting, but they have been asking us a lot of questions about hunting. It would be awesome if Jack and his dad could come with us next year and we could show them how fun turkey hunting is.

"Hi Jack Man, this is Luke."

"What's up Luke, did you get a turkey?" Jack asked.

"You better believe it. And I wasn't the only one. My dad nailed a giant tom, too. We went two for two on giant gobblers! It was so cool, you should have been here. Please ask your dad if you guys can come next year; my dad said he'd love to have you guys join us."

"What would I have to do to get ready?" Jack asked.

"You and your dad can come to our cabin and we can show you how to shoot a gun. My dad is great at teaching gun safety and he can give you pointers on how to shoot a turkey. My dad and I will take you guys out and be your guides. I think it would be great to be with you when you get your first turkey. What do you say, Jack Man?"

"It sounds good to me! Hold on, Luke. *HEY DAD, LUKE AND HIS DAD WANT TO TAKE US TURKEY HUNTING NEXT YEAR, ARE WE IN?*" Jack yelled with his hand over the phone. After a minute, he was back. "Luke, my dad said we are in! He wants to have you guys over for dinner next week to hear all about your hunt and to get more details. He will call your dad on Monday to talk."

"Yes! That's great!" I answered Jack. "Dad, they're in! Jack's dad will call you on Monday to talk about it."

"Wonderful," Dad replied.

"I will talk to you later, Jack Man," I said into the phone.

"Okay Luke, congratulations on getting a turkey. Goodbye."

I can't wait to get Jack out hunting with us. I know he is going to have a great time whether we get a bird or not. It's just going to be cool sharing this great land with a good buddy. I can't wait to see his face when he hears that first turkey gobble.

We made our way around the back of the farm to where the trailer sat in the pitch dark. Dad cut the headlights and we both turned on our little flashlights. I let Dad lead the way into the dark trailer, staying close behind him with my flashlight glowing. He lit the lantern and the warm light filled the trailer. Dad carefully carried the lantern back to the bedroom and set it on the back ledge.

I was exhausted from the long day when I crawled into my sleeping bag. Dad cut the light and darkness filled the room. It was peaceful and quiet. "Good night buddy, it was a great day that I will remember for a long time," Dad said quietly.

"Me too, Dad. Thanks for bringing me along. Good night."

Snuggled in my sleeping bag, many thoughts floated through my mind. I pictured the whole family sitting around the table at Thanksgiving, watching my dad pull my turkey out of the oven. I smiled, thinking how proud I would be to know I had helped feed everyone. My smile grew as my thoughts shifted back to the hunt. I realized that my dream had come true. I was sitting next to Dad when the turkey came in, and I was lucky enough to get the shot.

About the author

Kevin Lovegreen was born, raised, and lives in Minnesota with his loving wife and two amazing children. Hunting, fishing, and the outdoors have always been a big part of his life. From chasing squirrels as a child to chasing elk as an adult, Kevin loves the thrill of hunting, but even more, he loves telling the stories of the adventure. Presenting at schools and connecting with kids about the outdoors, is one of his favorite things to do.

The Swamp
The Swamp Extended Ver.
Turkey Tales

To order the
Lucky Luke's Hunting Adventures Series
visit: **LuckyLukeHunting.com**